THE FLINTSTONES

THE FLINTSTONES STORYBOOK

Stories by Horace J. Elias

GROSSET & DUNLAP
A FILMWAYS COMPANY
Publishers · New York

Distributed by Grosset & Dunlap Inc.

Published by Ottenheimer Publishers, Inc.
Library of Congress Catalog Card No. 77-94035
ISBN: 0-448-14744-0
(Material in this book originally appeared in
THE FLINTSTONES: WILMA'S BUSY DAY; THE FLINTSTONES:
FRED'S BIG CLEANING DAY; THE FLINTSTONES: PEBBLES AND
BAMM-BAMM FIND THINGS TO DO; and THE FLINTSTONES; FRED
FLINTSTONE'S SURPRISING CORN.)

Contents

FRED'S BIG CLEANING DAY

If Fred Flintstone had known what was going to happen to him on that beautiful Sunday in late spring, he never would have gotten out of bed.

It all started quite peacefully. Fred got up early and decided to take a nice, long warm bath. Then he got dressed and went downstairs, got the Sunday Bedrock Bulletin from off the roof (for some reason, the delivery boy always managed to throw the Sunday paper on the roof), and settled down to read.

7

About an hour later, he heard Wilma and Pebbles moving around. It was then that he made his first mistake of the day.

"Everybody's up," he said to himself. "Why don't I be a real nice guy and fix breakfast for the three of us?"

Fred put down the paper, went to the kitchen, and got out the big bowl of fresh eggs. Just as he was about to set it down, Dino, the Flintstones' pet baby dinosaur, decided to wake up. Did you ever hear a rooster's wake-up crow? Dino made a waking-up sound, too, only it sounded like forty

YAWN-N-N

lions roaring at once, plus a jet engine in the next room, plus a trunk full of old iron and broken glass being bounced on a drum.

Fred jumped three feet straight up, the bowl went into the air, turned upside down, and two

dozen eggs landed on Fred's head.

About this time, Wilma came into the kitchen. She didn't yell at Fred, though. She just said, "Clean it up, Fred—I'll make pancakes for breakfast."

Fred got the mess in the kitchen cleaned up, went upstairs, took off his clothes, and had bath number two.

He made his second mistake right after the pancake breakfast, when he decided to stroll over to Barney Rubble's house for a visit. When he got

there, Betty Rubble told him Barney was out back, working on his rockmobile. Sure enough, Fred found Barney under the rockmobile, making loud, complaining noises.

"This bothersome thing is just too much!" yelled Barney. "Everytime I get it all together, something falls out!"

"My boy," said Fred, "you just don't have the knack. Get out of there and let a real mechanic take over. I'll have it fixed in no time!"

"If that's Fred Flintstone," snarled Barney from under the rockmobile, "just go away, will you? I've got enough trouble here without your ten thumbs getting in the way."

"Barney," replied Fred, "if you want to have it fixed, get out of there now and let the master take over!"

14

"Okay, wise guy," growled Barney as he crawled out, "but make it snappy. I've got to go to a meeting in half an hour!"

Fred took Barney's place underneath and saw what the trouble was right away. But he unbolted the wrong bolt, and the next thing he knew, he was drenched with about three quarts of black, greasy engine oil.

After the usual yelling back and forth about

whose fault it was, Fred made his way home for bath number three. When he got out of the tub, he said to himself, "I'm going to sit in a chair and do NOTHING for the rest of the day! Maybe that way I can stay clean!"

Just as he stepped out of the tub, he heard a

noise in Pebbles' room. It sounded like 'Glug-glug-glug.' Then he heard Pebbles say, "Da Da Goo Goo" three times, and start to cry. He dashed into Pebbles' room, and immediately slipped and slid across the room, hitting his head against the wall. He tried to get up, but he fell right down again. Then he looked around and saw an empty bottle of baby oil, while Pebbles and the floor were covered with the slippery stuff. Next, he looked at

17

himself and discovered that he was covered with oil, too. It was then that Wilma appeared in the doorway and remarked, "Fred, if you're going skating in Pebbles' bedroom, don't you think you'd better put some clothes on?"

Fred said, "Grrr!" a few times, picked up Pebbles, and got in the tub with her for bath

number four. But when he got out, he found himself still full of oil, because when the oil came off in the water, it floated on top and went right back on his skin as he got out!

This time, Fred wiped Pebbles and himself with towels to remove most of the baby oil, then got back into a fresh tub of water for bath number five.

By now, it was time for lunch. After lunch,

Wilma said, "Fred, dear, it's almost summer. We won't be using the fireplace anymore until the weather turns cold again. Could you close the damper on it so that the rain won't come in?"

Fred complained that it was Sunday, which was supposed to be a day of rest, but he finally got up, went to the fireplace, and looked up. At just that moment, a strong puff of wind came along and Fred backed out of the fireplace, coughing

20

and choking, covered from head to toe with the dirt and dust blown down the chimney by the wind!

Bath number six followed immediately. Wilma said, "Fred, your skin's getting all wrinkly. You're taking too many baths!"

Fred grunted, "One more bath and I won't HAVE any skin!"

"Let's take Pebbles for a walk. It's a beautiful day," suggested Wilma.

Fred supposed there was no way he could get dirty simply by taking a walk, so he agreed, and the three of them set out. Fifteen minutes later, Fred was back in the bathtub again for bath number seven. He had been walking nearest to

the street when a rockmobile, driving too fast, tore through a large puddle, covering Fred with muddy, greasy water!

Just before bedtime, Fred and Wilma heard Dino making strange sounds in the back yard, and when Fred went out to check up, he stumbled over what was causing the trouble—a skunk! It

23

took two baths in a row before Fred got the skunk
odor washed away!

Next day at the rock mine, Barney asked,
"What's wrong with you today, Fred? You've got
no pep. You're draggin' around like an old man!"

"Barney," answered Fred, "I'm not an old
man yet, but I'm all washed up!"

PEBBLES AND BAMM-BAMM FIND THINGS TO DO

Boys and girls sometimes get into trouble when they try to do things they've seen grown-ups do.

That's because they don't know how to do these things — they've only watched them being done.

That was how Pebbles and Bamm-Bamm got into trouble the day Wilma had to rush over to Betty Rubble's to help her hang some curtains in a hurry. Of course, Wilma made a big mistake, too — she left the children alone in the house.

It all began in the morning. Fred was shaving, getting ready to leave for work, when he got a rockaphone call to rush to the rock mine at once. He yelled something that sounded like, "Trouble at the mine — gotta go!" and dashed out of the house. He knocked his tube of shaving cream to the floor as he did so.

Then Betty brought Bamm-Bamm over to play with Pebbles so she could hang curtains in peace and quiet. But she couldn't quite get them hung right, so she called Wilma to come over and help

out. Wilma said, "Oh, dear! Yes, I'll be right over!" Then she turned to Pebbles and Bamm-Bamm, who were playing quietly in the living room, and said, "You two behave yourselves. I'll be right back!" Then SHE dashed out of the house.

As soon as she was gone, Pebbles looked at Bamm-Bamm, and Bamm-Bamm looked at Pebbles. They didn't say a word, but each knew what the other was thinking. It was, "Oh, boy! The house is ours! Let's go!"

They both scooted straight for the bathroom, and in no time at all, Pebbles had her mother's lipstick out and was busy trying to use it. Unfortunately, she got most of the red color on her nose, her forehead, and both hands.

Bamm-Bamm noticed the tube of shaving cream as soon as they got to the bathroom. It took him a little while to get the cap off, but when he did, he squeezed as hard as he could. A big white worm of shaving cream shot out of the tube.

33

Bamm-Bamm put his hands in it, and rubbed it on his face the way he'd seen his daddy do it. But since he'd only SEEN it done, his aim wasn't very good, and so he got it in his hair, his ears, and his mouth — just about everyplace but on his cheeks. Then he tried to wash it off, but all he did was

34

make it bubble up. In the meantime, Pebbles, trying to get the lipstick off her hands, smeared it all
over herself and the bathroom, too. Then the two

of them went back to the living room, with Bamm-Bamm still holding onto the tube of shaving cream.

It was then that Dino, the Flintstones' pet baby dinosaur, decided that he was lonesome all by

himself in the back yard, so he wandered into the house, looking for someone to play with. Bamm-Bamm gave the tube a big squeeze — and there was Dino, with a faceful of shaving cream!

Dino thought that was lots of fun. He began to

dance and prance around the room, making some
of the strange sounds that baby dinosaurs make.
The he reared back on his hind legs and let loose a
real roar, just as Wilma and Betty came walking
through the front door!

Wilma promptly fainted. Betty rushed to the rockaphone, got Fred on the line, and said, "Fred, you'd better get here in a big hurry! Pebbles has blood all over her, Dino's gone mad, Bamm-Bamm looks as if he's been in a blizzard, and Wilma's on the floor, unconscious!"

39

It took quite a while, but finally they were able to bring Wilma awake and clean up the two children and Dino. Betty took Bamm-Bamm home and Fred went back to work. Just as Bamm-Bamm went out the door, he looked at Pebbles, winked an eye at her, and said, "bamm bamm!" three times, which meant, "Thank you very much

40

for a wonderful time. Next time, come to MY house
and we'll REALLY have some fun!"

Pebbles said, "Da Da Goo Goo!" twice, which
meant, "It was a pleasure being with you. Next
time you come, I know where there's some lovely
shoe polish we can play with!"

41

WILMA'S
BUSY DAY

One morning, Wilma Flintstone sent Fred off to work at the rock mine, washed the breakfast dishes, got all the cleaning and dusting done, got everything together she was going to need to cook dinner, and flopped down in a chair in the living room. Pebbles was playing quietly in a corner of the room.

"I'm TIRED!" groaned Wilma. "But for a wonder, I've got things done early. I think I'll just go take my bath and relax! Pebbles, be a good little girl and don't get into any mischief while I'm in the tub!"

Pebbles said, "Da Da Goo Goo!"

Wilma went to the bathroom and ran some nice, warm water into the tub. But as she was about to step in, the rockaphone rang.

45

"Oh, piffle!" said Wilma. Then she went to answer the phone. It was her best friend, Betty Rubble, who wanted to talk about almost anything, as usual. Wilma finished her chitchat with Betty as soon as she could, but by the time she got back to the bathroom, the water was too cold. She let all the water run out, and then filled the tub with warm water again.

This time Wilma got one foot into the tub, when the doorbell rang. "Oh, my stars and bananas!" she cried in annoyance, and went to the front door to see who it was.

47

"Collecting for the Bedrock Bulletin!" said the young man at the door. Wilma asked how much she owed and then discovered that she didn't have enough change—and neither did the paper boy. Wilma waited while he went to the store to get change for her.

By the time everything straightened out,
Wilma returned to the bathroom, only to discover
the water was cold once again.

Wilma just stared at the tub for a minute, then
let all the water out and filled it for the third time.

She never had a chance to put even a toe in the water, though, because just as the tub was filled, she heard an earthshaking clatter and commotion coming from the back yard.

Wilma dashed outside in time to see Dino, the

Flintstones' pet baby dinosaur, racing around and around a tree and roaring with every turn. She looked up in the tree that Dino was circling, and there, at the very top, was a squirrel!

It took a while to convince Dino that a squirrel wasn't really worth much noise and excitement. And when Wilma got back to the bathroom, guess what? Right! The water was cold again!

"Oh, dear, and a bushel of cornflakes!" sighed Wilma. "I wonder if I'll EVER get a bath today?" She let out all the water, and tried again. But just as she turned on the faucet to fill the tub for a fourth time, the rockaphone rang again!

Wilma raced to the rockaphone to answer it, and when she did, a voice at the other end said, "Is that you, Wilma? This is Betty. I didn't want you,

I must have the wrong number. I was calling the plumber, because our bathtub has sprung a leak and I want to take a bath!"

Wilma said, "So do I, Betty dear. GOOD-BYE!" She hung up the phone and started for the bathroom just as the doorbell rang again. When

55

she went to the door, a young man greeted her saying, "Good morning. I'm selling subscriptions to magazines, and if I sell enough of them, I get to go to college. Would you like to subscribe to almost any magazine at all?"

"I have all the magazines I need, thank you,"
answered Wilma politely.

"But I can offer you something special today,"
said the young man. "How would you like — ."

"Oh! Oh!" shrieked Wilma. "Good-bye! I just

remembered I LEFT THE WATER RUNNING
IN THE TUB!" She slammed the front door and
flew upstairs. The tub was just about to spill over!

"Oof!" said Wilma as she reached over to turn
off the water. "One more minute and we'd have
had a flood! I'll just let some of the water out until

it's the right level for me."

While she was standing there, watching the water slowly run out, a crash was heard in the living room. She dashed there as quickly as she could and discovered a lamp knocked off the table, broken glass all over, and Pebbles crying.

Wilma gathered up the broken bits of glass, put the broken lamp aside, and picked up Pebbles.

"C'mon, baby," said Wilma wearily. "It's time for your lunch, your bath, and your nap. I hope you'll have better luck than I did!"

FRED FLINTSTONE'S SURPRISING CORN

One sunny Sunday in the month of June, Fred
Flintstone finished a late breakfast and said to
Wilma, "You know what? I'm gonna grow some
corn this summer! I love corn on the cob, with lots
of butter and salt, and this summer, instead of
going to the store to buy it, I'd like to go out in the
yard and PICK it!"

"Goodness, Fred!" exclaimed Wilma. "Are you

62

SURE you want to bother? You have to dig all those holes in the ground, and plant the seed, and cover it, and hoe it, and water it, and weed it, and I don't know what all!"

"Nonsense!" grunted Fred. "Every time I want to do something, you make it sound impossible. Corn practically grows by itself! Just stick it in the ground and wait for it to come up!"

"Where are you going to get the corn kernels to plant?" asked Wilma.

"What's corn kernels?" asked Fred.

"It's like little bitty pieces of corn you put in the ground. That's what the corn grows from!" replied Wilma.

"Oh, those things! Barney's got some he saved from last year," said Fred. "I'm going over there now and get them from him."

65

A little while later, Fred came back from Barney's house, carrying a bag full of kernels of corn.

"Where are you going to plant it, Fred?" asked Wilma.

"Right in the front yard!" replied Fred. "There's that bare place where we can't get any grass to grow. That way I won't have to take any grass off to get down to the dirt. And besides, I want to be able to see it growing when I go out in the morning and come home at night. Here we go!"

Fred went out front, looked at his garden tools, and then said to himself, "Why do all that work? I'll just get a sharp stick and make a little scratch in the ground, plant the corn in the scratch, sweep the dirt back over it, and that'll do it!"

Wilma could hear him as he began to plant. He sang a few songs as he worked, making them up as he went along.

Like: "All I'll do is plant this corn. Then sit down
while it gets born!"

And: "Plant this stuff — that's all you do — Then corn on the cob! Yabba dabba doo!"

Next morning, Fred left for work. When he walked through the front yard, he said, "Good morning, corn on the cob! See you later!" When he came home that evening, he said, "Howdy do, corn! See you in the morning."

Fred didn't know it, but he had made a big mistake. He hadn't planted the corn deep enough. The mistake, and the hottest weather Bedrock had EVER had, caused some strange things to happen in the Flintstones' front yard.

By Thursday, the heat wave was so bad the owner of the rock mine told everybody to stay home the next day. It was just too hot to work.

So Friday, instead of going to work, Fred stayed home. Barney, his neighbor, came over and the two men had an argument about whether it was

too hot to go fishing. They finally decided it wasn't worth the trouble. After lunch, Fred and Barney went out front to cool off and Fred said, "Let's see how my corn's doing."

They walked to where Fred had planted the kernels.

"I don't see a thing," said Barney.

Fred bent over to take a closer look. Suddenly, there was a snapping noise, and something hit Fred in the eye. "Ouch!" he yelled. "What hit me?"

Barney bent over and looked. Another snapping noise, and Barney let loose a yell, too! Then,
there was a whole string of noises! It sounded like
someone shooting a cap pistol!

"What's going on here? Who's shooting? What's that white stuff?" hollered Fred.

"I'm not sure, Freddy, my boy," said Barney. "But I think you just became the first person in the world to GROW popcorn!"

78

79